First American Edition 2020
Kane Miller, A Division of EDC Publishing

First published in Great Britain 2019 by Alanna Max,
38 Oakfield Road, London N4 4NL, UK.
Lenny and Wilbur copyright © Alanna Max 2019
Text and illustrations copyright © Ken Wilson-Max 2019
The moral rights of the author/illustrator have been asserted.

For information contact:
Kane Miller, A Division of EDC Publishing
P.O. Box 470663
Tulsa, OK 74147-0663
www.kanemiller.com
www.edcpub.com
www.usbornebooksandmore.com

Library of Congress Control Number: 2019943391

Printed and bound in China
1 2 3 4 5 6 7 8 9 10
ISBN: 978-1-68464-071-3
Illustrated with acrylic.

Ken Wilson-Max

Lenny and Wilbur

Kane Miller
A DIVISION OF EDC PUBLISHING

Lenny and Wilbur are
the best of friends.

**Best friends
have fun together!**

It's Wilbur's bath day today!
"Ask him to sit," Mommy says.

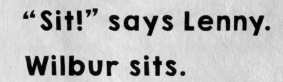

"Sit!" says Lenny.
Wilbur sits.

**First some warm water
to wet his fur.**

"Then shampoo,
to wash it clean,"
says Mommy.

Wilbur shakes.
Lenny giggles.

Best friends
laugh together!

Lenny rubs
Wilbur's tummy
and brushes
his fur.

Wilbur gets a treat.
"Good doggy!" says Mommy.
"Good doggy!" says Lenny.

Best friends eat together.

"Good boy, Lenny!" says Mommy.

"Good boy, Wilbur!" says Lenny.

Wilbur tickles Lenny's ear.
Is it time for a song?

Old McDonald had a farm
Hee-hi hee-hi ho!

And on that farm he had a dog
Hee-hi hee-hi ho!

With a Woof Woof here
And a Woof Woof there

Here a Woof, there a Woof
Everywhere a Woof Woof!

Old McDonald had a farm
Hee-hi hee-hi ho!

When they are finally tired,
best friends rest together.